I, TOO, SING AMERICA

Three Centuries of African American Poetry

811
I   I, too, sing
           America.

Hammond High School

15BT01350

$20.00

DATE			

I, TOO, SING AMERICA
Three Centuries of African American Poetry

Catherine Clinton

Illustrated by Stephen Alcorn

Houghton Mifflin Company
Boston 1998

for Ned and Margaret Colbert
– C. C.

for Lucrezia, as she comes of age
– S. A.

Copyright © 1998 by Catherine Clinton
Illustrations and Illustrator's Note Copyright © 1998 by Stephen Alcorn

All rights reserved. For information about permission to reproduce selections from this book, write to
Permissions, Houghton Mifflin Company, 215 Park Avenue South, New York, New York 10003.

The text of this book is set in Adobe Minion.
The illustrations are mixed media on paper.

Library of Congress Cataloging-in-Publication Data

I, too, sing America : three centuries of African American poetry /
selected and annotated by Catherine Clinton ; illustrated by Stephen Alcorn.
p. cm.
ISBN 0-395-89599-5
1. Children's poetry, American—Afro-American authors.
2. Afro-Americans—Juvenile poetry. I. Clinton, Catherine, 1952–   . II. Alcorn, Stephen.
PS591.N4I35   1998
712.2—dc21   97-46137 CIP

Printed in Singapore
TWP 10 9 8 7 6 5 4 3 2

Acknowledgments

Acknowledgment is made to the following publishers and authors or their representatives for their permission to use copyrighted material. Every reasonable effort has been made to clear the use of the poems in this volume with the copyright owners. If notified of any omissions, the editor and publisher will gladly make the proper corrections in future printings.

Broadside Press, Detroit, MI, for "Martin Luther King, Jr." by Gwendolyn Brooks.

Gwendolyn Brooks for "Malcolm X" and "We Real Cool" from *Blacks* by Gwendolyn Brooks. Copyright © 1991 by Gwendolyn Brooks, published by Third World Press, Chicago.

Harcourt Brace & Company for "Women" from *Revolutionary Petunias & Other Poems,* copyright © 1970 by Alice Walker, reprinted by permission of Harcourt Brace & Company.

Alfred A. Knopf, Inc., for "I, Too," "Harlem," "The Negro Speaks of Rivers," "Merry Go Round," and "Cross" from *Collected Poems* by Langston Hughes. Copyright © 1994 by the Estate of Langston Hughes. Reprinted by permission of Alfred A. Knopf, Inc.

Liveright Publishing Corporation for "Beehive" from *Cane* by Jean Toomer. Copyright © 1923 by Boni & Liveright, copyright © renewed 1951 by Jean Toomer. Reprinted by permission of Liveright Publishing Corporation.

Permission pending for "If We Must Die" and "The White House" by Claude McKay.

William Morrow & Company, Inc., for "The Funeral of Martin Luther King, Jr." from *Black Feeling, Black Talk, Black Judgment,* by Nikki Giovanni. Copyright © 1968, 1970 by Nikki Giovanni. Reprinted by permission of William Morrow & Co., Inc.

W. W. Norton & Company for "Primer" from *Mother Love* by Rita Dove. Copyright © 1995 by Rita Dove. Reprinted by permission of W. W. Norton & Company.

W. W. Norton & Company for "Rites of Passage" from *The Collected Poems of Audre Lorde* by Audre Lorde. Copyright © 1976 by Audre Lorde. Reprinted by Permission of W. W. Norton & Company.

Harold Ober Associates Incorporated for "A Black Man Talks of Reaping" by Arna Bontemps. Copyright © 1963 by Arna Bontemps. Reprinted by permission of Harold Ober Associates Incorporated.

Penguin Books USA Inc. for "Lift Every Voice and Sing" from *Saint Peter Relates an Incident* by James Weldon Johnson. Copyright © 1917, 1921, 1935 by James Weldon Johnson, copyright © renewed 1963 by Grace Nail Johnson. Used by permission of Viking Penguin, a division of Penguin Books USA Inc.

Random House, Inc., for "Still I Rise" from *And Still I Rise* by Maya Angelou. Copyright © 1978 by Maya Angelou. Reprinted by permission of Random House, Inc.

Thompson and Thompson for "Tableau," "Saturday's Child," and "Incident" by Countee Cullen, published in *Color* by Harper & Bros., in 1925 and publication renewed in 1952 by Ida Cullen. Copyrights held by the Amistad Research Center, Administrated by Thompson and Thompson, New York, NY.

The University of Georgia Press for "Sorrow Home" from *This Is My Century: New and Collected Poems* by Margaret Walker Alexander.

University Press of Virginia for "We Wear the Mask" by Paul Laurence Dunbar from *The Collected Poetry of Paul Laurence Dunbar,* Joanne M. Braxton, ed. (Charlottesville: Virginia, 1993). Reprinted with permission of the University Press of Virginia.

CONTENTS

I, TOO, SING AMERICA
Langston Hughes

I, too, sing America.

I am the darker brother.
They send me to eat in the kitchen
When company comes,
But I laugh,
And eat well,
And grow strong.

Tomorrow,
I'll sit at the table
When company comes.
Nobody'll dare
Say to me,
"Eat in the kitchen,"
Then.

Besides,
They'll see how beautiful I am
And be ashamed—

I, too, am America.

Introduction

WHETHER BLENDED INTO THE GLORIOUS HARMONY OF gospel, forging the distinctive sounds of jazz, or raised in a familiar chorus of protest, African American voices reflect diverse contributions to our cultural heritage. Black poets, too, sing America.

Those who arrived on American shores in bondage were determined to break the chains, to force America to honor its pledge of justice and freedom for all. Enslaved Africans and their descendants challenged those who would deny them liberty—by any means necessary, including poetry.

The colonial poet Phillis Wheatley's verses were so skilled that many of her contemporaries argued they could not have been written by an African-born enslaved woman. When she finally proved to an audience of examiners that her poems were indeed "written by herself," her triumph over racism was a bittersweet victory, as she died impoverished and forgotten. A generation later, the North Carolina slave poet Moses Horton, denied by law his right to read and write, recited his poems from memory to a white audience who copied them down and paid him. The poet Claude McKay vowed during the Harlem Renaissance in the 1920s that blacks who continued to fight for equality might die, but at least they would die trying to make their voices heard.

Caught within the web of monumental and competing strug-gles — to write, to survive, to be heard, to be appreciated — African American poets created an impressive body of work. The selections that follow reflect themes of exclusion, tales of discrimination, and the inspiring talents of black poets stretching from the first half of the eighteenth century until the final years of the twentieth. Brief biographies of each poet, especially those born in earlier centuries, reveal the ways in which race may have dictated the terms of a poet's literary career. Many insisted upon "singing America" even while whites turned a deaf ear.

Yet the gifts of individual poets are increasingly acknowledged: the writers in this collection include three Pulitzer Prize winners (two in poetry) and one former poet laureate of the United States. Nevertheless, even the most honored of African American poets may remind us that the struggle continues. As we each seek our own voice, as we look to the past and anticipate the future, the power and promise of these verses encourage us. If we let the voices of the poets get through to us, then maybe one day we can all find a way to sing America together.

LUCY TERRY

(1730-1821)

BORN IN AFRICA, LUCY TERRY WAS KIDNAPPED AT A YOUNG AGE AND brought to Rhode Island, where she was sold into slavery. In 1735 Ebenezer Wells purchased her to become his servant in Deerfield, Massachusetts. Her rhymed account of an Indian raid in 1746, "Bars Fight," is the first poem known to be composed by an African American. When Terry was twenty-six, Obijah Prince, a free black, bought her freedom and married her. In 1760 the couple moved to Guilford, Vermont, where Terry raised her six children and became a famous storyteller. After her husband died in 1794, she lived a hardscrabble life until her death more than twenty-five years later. Terry's fame survived her lifetime: "Bars Fight" was passed down orally for generations until it was finally published in 1855. Today we can celebrate her as our first African American literary voice.

~

The ambush of two white families on the twenty-fifth of August, 1746, was not rare in colonial America. But it was a tragic event in the lives of the Deerfield community on the Massachusetts frontier, robbed of friends and neighbors who were slain by Indians in nearby meadowlands ("bars" was a colonial word for "meadows"). Terry most likely composed her verses to be sung, and her ballad first appeared in Josiah Holland's History of Western Massachusetts *(1855) as an example of regional folklore. As "Bars Fight" testifies, blacks were part of the American experience from the very beginning of our country's history.*

BARS FIGHT

August, 'twas the twenty-fifth,
Seventeen hundred forty-six,
The Indians did in ambush lay,
Some very valient men to slay,
The names of whom I'll not leave out:
Samuel Allen like a hero fout,
And though he was so brave and bold,
His face no more shall we behold.

Eleazer Hawks was killed outright,
Before he had time to fight,—
Before he did the Indians see,
Was shot and killed immediately.

Oliver Amsden he was slain,
Which caused his friends much grief and pain.
Simeon Amsden they found dead
Not many rods distant from his head.
Adonijah Gillett, we do hear,
Did lose his life which was so dear.
John Sadler fled across the water.
And thus escaped the dreadful slaughter.

Eunice Allen see the Indians coming,
And hopes to save herself by running;
And had not her petticoats stopped her,
The awful creatures had not catched her.
Nor tommy hawked her on the head,
And left her on the ground for dead.
Young Samuel Allen, Oh, lack-a-day!
Was taken and carried to Canada.

PHILLIS WHEATLEY

(1753-1784)

PHILLIS WHEATLEY EARNED BOTH HER FREEDOM FROM SLAVERY AND A WIDE literary following with her poetry. This young girl from Gambia was sold on the auction block in Boston before the age of nine. She was called Phillis (the name of the ship on which she came from Africa) by her owner, John Wheatley, who bought her to serve as his wife's maid.

Within four years Phillis Wheatley could read and write, and at fourteen she published her first verse. She was soon studying Latin, encouraged in her literary pursuits and education by her mistress. Through the help of an admiring patron, she secured a publisher in London for a book of verse, *Poems on Various Subjects*. She also spent some time in England in 1773, shortly before her volume appeared. Wheatley's work was praised by leading figures of the day, including Benjamin Franklin, Voltaire, and George Washington. Although Wheatley was emancipated in 1773, she continued to live with her former owners until March 1778, when John Wheatley died.

A month later she wed John Peters, a free black Boston tradesman. Marriage curtailed her publishing, if not her writing, for the next five years. The couple was living in poverty when three elegies and the poem "Liberty and Peace" appeared in 1784. Wheatley announced another volume of poems, but she died in December 1784, before it was completed.

Wheatley was a pioneering poet—the first African American and only the second woman in the American colonies to publish a book. In her own lifetime, her remarkable gifts gained her fame, and she was the first black poet in the world to attain an international literary reputation.

❧

Wheatley turned her poetic imagination to patriotism as early as 1770, when she wrote a verse celebrating the heroism of Crispus Attucks's death at the Boston Massacre. In a letter printed in a newspaper in 1774 she declared that within every human "Love of Freedom . . . is impatient of Oppression, and pants for Deliverance." With the Declaration of Independence in 1776 and the war against Britain, America became a new nation, and Wheatley was caught up in the spirit of the times. The last poem she ever published, "Liberty and Peace," reflected her dedication to the principles that fueled the American Revolution and the antislavery movement, which blossomed after her death in 1784.

LIBERTY AND PEACE

LO! Freedom comes. Th' prescient Muse foretold,
    All Eyes th' accomplish'd Prophecy behold:
Her Port describ'd, *"She moves divinely fair,*
"Olive and Laurel bind her golden Hair."
She, the bright Progeny of Heaven, descends,
And every Grace her sovereign Step attends;
For now kind Heaven, indulgent to our Prayer,
In smiling *Peace* resolves the Din of *War.*
Fix'd in *Columbia* her illustrious Line,
And bids in thee her future Councils shine.
To every Realm her Portals open'd wide,
Receives from each the full commercial Tide.
Each Art and Science now with rising Charms
Th' expanding Heart with Emulation warms.
E'en great *Britannia* sees with dread Surprize,
And from the dazzl'ing Splendor turns her Eyes!
Britain, whose Navies swept th' *Atlantic* o'er,
And Thunder sent to every distant Shore:
E'en thou, in Manners cruel as thou art,
The Sword resign'd, resume the friendly Part!
For *Galia's* Power espous'd *Columbia's* Cause,
And new-born *Rome* shall give *Britannia* Law,
Nor unremember'd in the grateful Strain,
Shall princely *Louis'* friendly Deeds remain;
The generous Prince th' impending Vengeance eye's,
Sees the fierce Wrong, and to the rescue flies.
Perish that Thirst of boundless Power, that drew
On *Albion's* Head the Curse to Tyrants due.
But thou appeas'd submit to Heaven's decree,
That bids this Realm of Freedom rival thee!
Now sheathe the Sword that bade the Brave attone
With guiltless Blood for Madness not their own.
Sent from th' Enjoyment of their native Shore
Ill-fated—never to behold her more!
From every Kingdom on *Europa's* Coast
Throng'd various Troops, their Glory, Strength and Boast.

With heart-felt pity fair *Hibernia* saw
Columbia menac'd by the Tyrant's Law:
On hostile Fields fraternal Arms engage,
And mutual Deaths, all dealt with mutual Rage;
The Muse's Ear hears mother Earth deplore
Her ample Surface smoak with kindred Gore:
The hostile Field destroys the social Ties,
And ever-lasting Slumber seals their Eyes.
Columbia mourns, the haughty Foes deride,
Her Treasures plunder'd, and her Towns destroy'd:
Witness how *Charlestown's* curling Smoaks arise,
In sable Columns to the clouded Skies!
The ample Dome, high-wrought with curious Toil,
In one sad Hour the savage Troops despoil.
Descending *Peace* and Power of War confounds;
From every Tongue celestial *Peace* resounds:
As for the East th' illustrious King of Day,
With rising Radiance drives the Shades away,
So Freedom comes array'd with Charms divine,
And in her Train Commerce and Plenty shine.
Britannia owns her Independent Reign,
Hibernia, Scotia, and the Realms of *Spain;*
And great *Germania's* ample Coast admires
The generous Spirit that *Columbia* fires.
Auspicious Heaven shall fill with fav'ring Gales,
Where e'er *Columbia* spreads her swelling Sails:
To every Realm shall *Peace* her Charms display,
And Heavenly *Freedom* spread her golden Ray.

GEORGE MOSES HORTON

(1797-1883)

BORN A SLAVE ON A TOBACCO FARM IN RURAL NORTH CAROLINA, GEORGE Moses Horton began to compose verses in his head while still an illiterate teenager. Though denied an education, he was allowed by his master to visit the University of North Carolina nearby. He would recite his poems to students, who eagerly wrote them down and paid him for his compositions. His fame spread, and a collection of poems was published under the title *The Hope of Liberty* (1829). Horton was the first black southern author and the first African American poet to produce a volume in more than half a century.

Horton's master permitted him to support himself by his writing, but he refused to allow Horton's patrons to purchase his freedom. Disappointed, Horton learned to write for himself and continued to publish, producing a second volume, *Poetical Works* (1845) and calling himself "the Colored Bard of North Carolina." His third and final volume, *Naked Genius,* appeared in 1865. Horton's literary attacks on slavery were dynamic, vivid, and powerful. After the Civil War, he moved to Philadelphia, where he lived until his death. Once in the North, he never published another verse, having retired from his role as "the slave poet."

~

As a poet, Horton was praised and published for over a quarter of a century before he was liberated by Union troops in 1865. He celebrated his release from what he called his "loathesome fetters," by publishing his first collection as a free man: Naked Genius. *A recurrent theme of his published work, the agony of bondage and the desire for liberty, is revealed in his poem "On Liberty and Slavery."*

ON LIBERTY AND SLAVERY

Alas! and am I born for this,
    To wear this slavish chain?
Deprived of all created bliss,
    Through hardship, toil and pain!

How long have I in bondage lain,
    And languished to be free!
Alas! and must I still complain—
    Deprived of liberty.

Oh, Heaven! and is there no relief
    This side the silent grave—
To soothe the pain—to quell the grief
    And anguish of a slave?

Come, Liberty, thou cheerful sound,
    Roll through my ravished ears!
Come, let my grief in joys be drowned,
    And drive away my fears.

Say unto foul oppression, Cease:
    Ye tyrants rage no more,
And let the joyful trump of peace,
    Now bid the vassal soar.

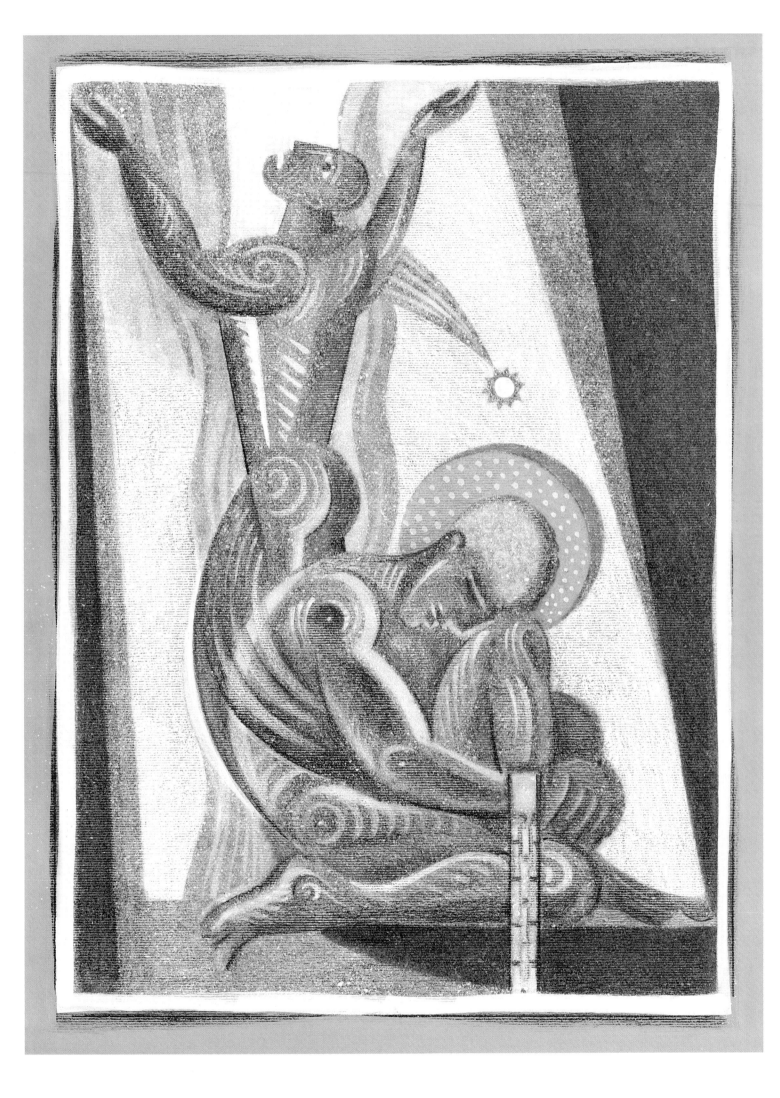

JAMES M. WHITFIELD

(1822–1871)

LITTLE IS KNOWN ABOUT JAMES M. WHITFIELD'S EARLY LIFE EXCEPT THAT HE was born in New Hampshire. He was working in a barber shop in Buffalo in the 1840s, cutting hair by day and writing poetry at night, when he met the legendary black abolitionist Frederick Douglass. Douglass was happy to feature Whitfield's verse in the antislavery newspaper he edited in Rochester, New York, the *North Star*. The paper was named after the landmark star that fugitive slaves learned to follow to reach freedom. Whitfield celebrated themes of freedom in his verse, and his first book of poetry was published in 1853. He migrated to San Francisco, where he continued to work as a barber while publishing his poetry in newspapers in California. Unable to trade in his scissors for his pen to earn a living, Whitfield never gained fame or recognition during his own lifetime. Nevertheless, his poetry sings for us still.

Many of Whitfield's verses were full of bitterness and anger at the world. Certainly Whitfield resented discrimination against African Americans, and he became involved with the Back to Africa movement launched by blacks who felt they would never be treated equally in the United States. Whitfield felt alienated from his homeland because of the raw nerve of racism that permeated politics both North and South. One powerful poem, "Yes! Strike Again That Sounding String," reflects his strong belief that an artist must use gifts of the imagination to drive away the demons—to overcome the melancholy that too many black poets experienced as they struggled in their role as writers.

YES! STRIKE AGAIN THAT SOUNDING STRING

Yes! strike again that sounding string,
    And let the wildest numbers roll;
Thy song of fiercest passion sing—
    It breathes responsive to my soul!

A soul, whose gentlest hours were nursed,
    In stern adversity's dark way,
And o'er whose pathway never burst
    One gleam of hope's enlivening ray.

If thou wouldst soothe my burning brain.
    Sing not to me of joy and gladness;
'Twill but increase the raging pain.
    And turn the fever into madness.

Sing not to me of landscapes bright,
    Of fragrant flowers and fruitful trees—
Of azure skies and mellow light,
    Or whisperings of the gentle breeze;

But tell me of the tempest roaring
    Across the angry foaming deep,
Or torrents from the mountains pouring
    Down precipices dark and steep.

Sing of the lightning's lurid flash,
    The ocean's roar, the howling storm,
The earthquake's shock, the thunder's crash,
    Where ghastly terrors teeming swarm.

Sing of the battle's deadly strife,
    The ruthless march of war and pillage,
The awful waste of human life,
    The plundered town, the burning village!

Of streets with human gore made red,
  Of priests upon the altar slain;
The scenes of rapine, woe and dread,
  That fill the warrior's horrid train.

Thy song may then an echo wake,
  Deep in this soul, long crushed and sad,
The direful impressions shake
  Which threaten now to drive it mad.

FRANCES ELLEN WATKINS HARPER
(1825-1911)

FRANCES ELLEN WATKINS HARPER WAS A POPULAR AND PROLIFIC WRITER who earned praise for her novels, short stories, and essays, as well as several volumes of poetry. Born to free blacks in Maryland, she was orphaned at a young age. She attended her uncle's Academy for Negro Youth in Baltimore before moving to Ohio in 1850 to become the first female teacher at a seminary, which later became Wilberforce University. She moved to Philadelphia in 1853 and devoted her energies to the Underground Railroad and social reform.

Her first known book of poems, *Forest Leaves* (1854), has not survived, but her second, *Poems on Miscellaneous Subjects* (1854), sold ten thousand copies in its first printing and was reprinted twenty times during her lifetime. Harper continued to publish verse in anti-slavery journals after her marriage in 1860. Following her husband's death in 1864, she made extensive speaking tours throughout the South, encouraging blacks to demand fairness during Reconstruction and pushing for the vote for women. In 1896 she was one of the founding members of the National Association of Colored Women. When she died in 1911, she was lauded both for her distinguished literary reputation and her role as a civic activist.

Harper was not only the first but also the best known of the nineteenth century's African American "protest poets," who used their verse to advance political causes. During the antebellum era, Harper combined her literary interests and political causes, working to end slavery. She was caught up in historic events when John Brown led an integrated band of freedom fighters in a raid on Harpers Ferry, Virginia, in October 1859. Harper pledged her solidarity with Brown's cause and moved in with his wife to help her through both the death of her son in the failed raid and her husband's trial and execution. Harper wrote a letter to one of the condemned African American men who also was sentenced to die for his role in Brown's operation, enclosing "Bury Me in a Free Land." Along with "The Slave Mother" and the "Slave Auction," it provided Americans with dramatic eyewitness accounts of the evils of slavery.

BURY ME IN A FREE LAND

Make me a grave where'er you will,
In a lowly plain or a lofty hill;
Make it among earth's humblest graves,
But not in a land where men are slaves.

I could not rest, if around my grave
I heard the steps of a trembling slave;
His shadow above my silent tomb
Would make it a place of fearful gloom.

I could not sleep, if I heard the tread
Of a coffle-gang to the shambles led,
And the mother's shriek of wild despair
Rise, like a curse, on the trembling air.

I could not rest, if I saw the lash
Drinking her blood at each fearful gash;
And I saw her babes torn from her breast,
Like trembling doves from their parent nest.

I'd shudder and start, if I heard the bay
Of a bloodhound seizing his human prey;
And I heard the captive plead in vain,
As they bound, afresh, his galling chain.

If I saw young girls from their mother's arms
Bartered and sold for their youthful charms,
My eye would flash with a mournful flame,
My death-pale cheek grow red with shame.

I would sleep, dear friends, where bloated Might
Can rob no man of his dearest right;
My rest shall be calm in any grave
Where none can call his brother a slave.

I ask no monument, proud and high,
To arrest the gaze of the passers by;
All that my yearning spirit craves
Is—*Bury me not in a land of slaves!*

W.E.B. DU BOIS

(1868-1963)

W. E. B. DU BOIS WAS THE MOST INFLUENTIAL WRITER OF HIS GENERATION, A towering intellect whose work in African American arts and letters remains unsurpassed. Known for his scholarship, he also published fiction and poetry.

Raised by his mother in Great Barrington, Massachusetts, after his father deserted the family, Du Bois racked up an impressive list of degrees before the age of thirty: a B.A. from Fisk University in 1888 and an M.A. and a doctorate from Harvard by 1895. He published his first book in 1896, the same year he married and accepted a research position at the University of Pennsylvania. In 1897 he went to teach at the predominantly black Atlanta University, where he remained for over ten years and published the book for which he is best known today, *The Souls of Black Folk* (1903).

He began publishing poetry and moved to New York, where many black writers were involved in what became known as the Harlem Renaissance. In 1910 Du Bois assumed the editorship of *Crisis*, published by the National Association for the Improvement of Colored People (NAACP), which he had helped to establish. In 1920 he was among those who started a magazine for black children called *The Brownie's Book*.

Until he moved to Ghana in 1961, Du Bois remained active in the political struggle for African American equality. During his final years in Africa, he continued his commitment to anticolonialism and social justice.

When Du Bois died in 1963, he left behind several pioneering books of scholarship as well as half a dozen novels, several collections of essays, three autobiographies, and his poetry.

~

In "The Song of the Smoke," W. E. B. Du Bois presented new and interesting metaphors, transforming familiar notions of black and white, conjuring majestic visions, playing with words to create an alternative to racism: his images are black and powerful and positive. He turned to poetry to express his growing dissatisfaction with American race relations and to widen his circle of readers by exploring other literary genres.

THE SONG OF THE SMOKE

I am the Smoke King
I am black!
I am swinging in the sky,
I am wringing worlds awry;
I am the thought of the throbbing mills,
I am the soul of the soul-toil kills,
Wrath of the ripple of trading rills;
Up I'm curling from the sod,
I am whirling home to God;
I am the Smoke King
I am black.

I am the Smoke King,
I am black!
I am wreathing broken hearts,
I am sheathing love's light darts;
Inspiration of iron times
Wedding the toil of toiling climes,
Shedding the blood of bloodless crimes—
Lurid lowering 'mid the blue,
Torrid towering toward the true,
I am the Smoke King,
I am black.

I am the Smoke King,
I am black!
I am darkening with song,
I am hearkening to wrong!
I will be black as blackness can—
The blacker the mantle, the mightier the man!
For blackness was ancient ere whiteness began.
I am daubing God in night
I am swabbing Hell in white:
I am the Smoke King
I am black.
I am the Smoke King,
I am black!

I am cursing ruddy morn,
I am hearsing hearts unborn:
   Souls unto me are as stars in a night,
       I whiten my black men—I blacken my white!
       What's the hue of a hide to a man in his might?
Hail! great, gritty, grimy hands—
Sweet Christ, pity toiling lands!
        I am the Smoke King
        I am black.

JAMES WELDON JOHNSON

(1871–1938)

JAMES WELDON JOHNSON WAS A PROLIFIC AUTHOR WHOSE TALENTS WENT well beyond poetry. The oldest child of a mother who was a teacher and a father who was a headwaiter, he had a restless energy that launched him in several colorful careers over his lifetime.

After graduating from Atlanta University in 1894, Johnson returned home to Jacksonville, Florida, to head the Stanton School, which he himself had attended. At the same time, he edited a black community newspaper and launched his law practice. In 1901 he and his brother, the composer Rosamond Johnson, headed for New York to become a songwriting team.

In 1904 J. W. Johnson abandoned songwriting to study literature, and an appointment as U.S. consul to Venezuela in 1906 gave him the chance to live overseas. He also completed his first novel while abroad, *Autobiography of an Ex–Colored Man,* which he published anonymously in 1912.

Returning home in 1909, he devoted himself to literature and edited books of poetry, collected spirituals for anthologies, and published his own volume of poetry, *God's Trombones* (1927). In the 1930s he became a professor of literature at Fisk University in Nashville until his death in an automobile accident in 1938.

~

In February 1900 Johnson wrote "Lift Ev'ry Voice and Sing," which was set to music by his brother Rosamond to celebrate Lincoln's birthday at a school celebration. Although the brothers thought nothing more about the song after they published it, their students kept the words and music alive. Finally, in 1920 the NAACP adopted this popular anthem as the "Negro National Hymn." These forgotten verses became perhaps the most well known legacy of James Weldon Johnson, as young black voices have carried his words forward to symbolize African American pride for nearly a hundred years.

LIFT EV'RY VOICE AND SING

Lift ev'ry voice and sing,
Till earth and heaven ring,
Ring with the harmonies of Liberty;
Let our rejoicing rise
High as the list'ning skies,
Let it resound loud as the rolling sea.
Sing a song full of the faith that the dark past has taught us,
Sing a song full of the hope that the present has brought us;
Facing the rising sun of our new day begun,
Let us march on till victory is won.

Stony the road we trod,
Bitter the chast'ning rod,
Felt in the days when hope unborn had died;
Yet with a steady beat,
Have not our weary feet
Come to the place for which our fathers sighed?
We have come over a way that with tears has been watered,
We have come, treading our path through the blood of the
    slaughtered,
Out from the gloomy past,
Till now we stand at last
Where the white gleam of our bright star is cast.

God of our weary years,
God of our silent tears,
Thou who hast brought us thus far on the way;
Thou who hast by Thy might,
Led us into the light,
Keep us forever in the path, we pray.
Lest our feet stray from the places, our God, where we met Thee,
Lest our hearts, drunk with the wine of the world, we forget Thee;
Shadowed beneath Thy hand,
May we forever stand,
True to our God,
True to our native land.

PAUL LAURENCE DUNBAR

(1872-1906)

PAUL LAURENCE DUNBAR WROTE ELEVEN VOLUMES OF POETRY, INCLUDING his best-selling *Lyrics of Lowly Life* (1896), which gave him an international reputation and made him one of the most widely read black authors at the turn of the twentieth century. The African American leader Booker T. Washington proclaimed him "the Poet Laureate of the Negro race."

Born and raised in Dayton, Ohio, Dunbar was elected president of his senior class and read a poem at his high school graduation in 1891. Despite his talents, racial discrimination forced him to take a job as an elevator operator. He published his first collection of verse, *Oak and Ivy,* in 1893. His fame grew, and his dialect poetry (poems written in the spoken language of rural blacks) gained a wide following. In 1898 he married Alice Moore, a young black writer from New Orleans, and was offered a clerkship at the Library of Congress.

Dunbar began to expand his literary repertoire and published four novels and four collections of short stories over the next few years. His wife left him in 1902, after only four years of marriage. Dunbar had become addicted to the alcohol prescribed for his tuberculosis, from which he died in 1906.

Poets and critics of a later generation challenged Dunbar's extensive use of "Negro dialect," some condemning it as mere confirmation of racist stereotypes of African Americans rather than a celebration of folkways. But certainly no one could question that Dunbar produced powerful verses that confronted racism and affirmed black pride. One of his most significant nondialect poems on this theme was "We Wear the Mask." Dunbar skillfully used the image of disguise, the metaphor of a "mask," during the 1890s. It was one of the bloodiest periods of racial violence in American history, and many African Americans were forced to hide their feelings about segregation and inequality.

WE WEAR THE MASK

We wear the mask that grins and lies,
It hides our cheeks and shades our eyes,—
This debt we pay to human guile;
With torn and bleeding hearts we smile,
And mouth with myriad subtleties.

Why should the world be overwise,
In counting all our tears and sighs?
Nay, let them only see us, while
      We wear the mask.

We smile, but, O great Christ, our cries
To thee from tortured souls arise.
We sing, but oh the clay is vile
Beneath our feet, and long the mile;
But let the world dream otherwise,
      We wear the mask!

ANGELINA WELD GRIMKÉ

(1880-1958)

THE DAUGHTER OF A PROMINENT BLACK CLERGYMAN IN BOSTON, ANGELINA Weld Grimké was abandoned by her white mother at an early age. Raised by her father, she was named after his famous aunt, the remarkable white abolitionist feminist Angelina Grimké Weld. Because of her family's emphasis on education and reform, the girl attended excellent schools and her father pushed her to fulfill her potential. She wrote verse from an early age and published poems in her early twenties.

Shy about her creative abilities, in 1917 Grimké became an English teacher at the prestigious black Dunbar High School in Washington, D.C. Nevertheless, she wrote plays and continued to publish her poems. Grimké was one of the few black women writers to gain national renown—although her reputation was overshadowed by the male writers of the Harlem Renaissance. She never married and was devoted to her family and women friends, including Georgia Douglas Johnson, another poet in Washington.

After the death of her father in 1930, Grimké moved to Manhattan to pursue a writing career. However, she was lonely and published very little during the remainder of her life. Grimké died in 1958, unappreciated by all but a small circle of friends and fans.

~

Although she was not very prolific during her lifetime, Grimké enjoyed modest critical success during the Harlem Renaissance. Her verse appeared in several popular black journals and periodicals during the 1910s and '20s. Her poems often involved images of isolation, which echo an earlier shy and retiring woman poet, Emily Dickinson. Grimké's work also used color as a metaphor and is thought to have expressed her innermost feelings about race. "The Black Finger" reflects her spare and lyrical style. Grimké's verse has been rediscovered by a new generation of readers with critical reappraisal and renewed interest since the 1970s.

THE BLACK FINGER

I have just seen a beautiful thing
       Slim and still,
Against a gold, gold sky,
       A straight cypress,
       Sensitive
       Exquisite,
A black finger
Pointing upwards.
Why, beautiful, still finger are you black?
And why are you pointing upwards?

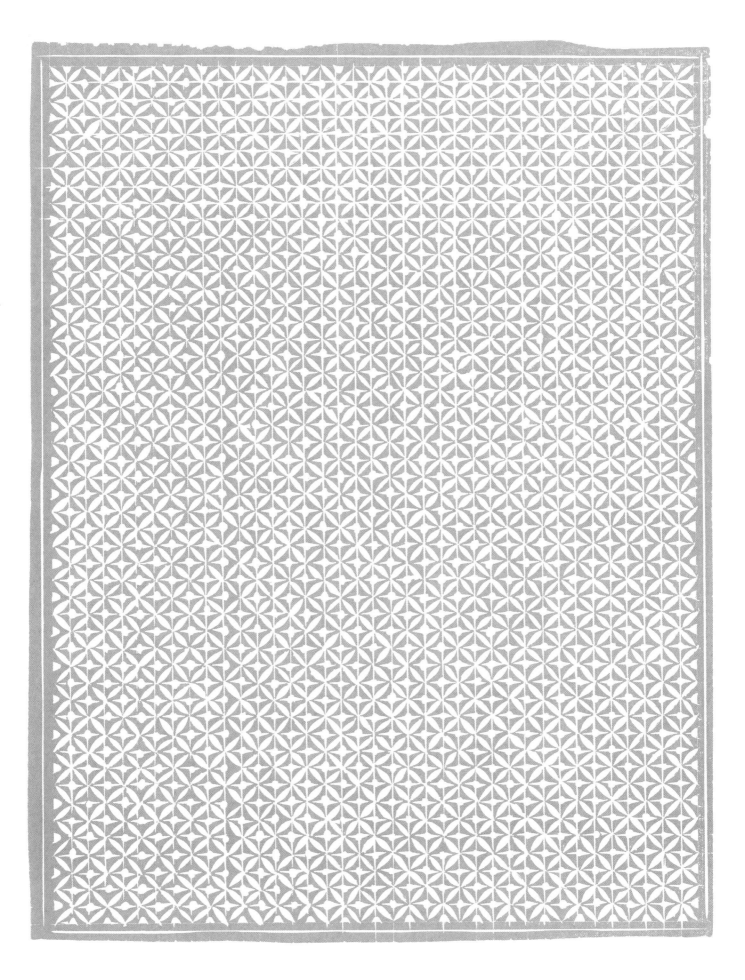

GEORGIA DOUGLAS JOHNSON

(1880-1966)

AS A YOUNG GIRL GROWING UP IN ROME, GEORGIA, GEORGIA DOUGLAS Johnson was encouraged to cultivate her writing talent. Later, she became a teacher and married an Atlanta University classmate, Henry Lincoln Johnson, in 1903. The couple moved to the nation's capital when her husband was offered a government appointment by President William H. Taft in 1912. As the wife of a Washington official and the mother of two, Johnson had little time for her writing; she published her first poem at the age of thirty-six. She then produced two volumes of poetry, *The Heart of a Woman* (1918) and *Bronze* (1922). Her husband's death in 1925 forced Johnson to take a series of jobs to support her teenage sons. During this period she published her best collection, *An Autumn Love Cycle* (1928). Johnson also created a literary salon, where Angelina Weld Grimké, Langston Hughes, Jean Toomer, and other poets might call during her weekly Saturday-night open house. She even took in writers down on their luck, calling her place "the Halfway House." Johnson also wrote a weekly newspaper column, "Homely Philosophy," syndicated in over a dozen newspapers from 1926 to 1932. Her fame spread as she lectured and toured during the Harlem Renaissance, and her success enabled her to send both her sons to Howard University. In her later years, she lived with her son Henry Lincoln, Jr., until her death in 1966.

~

Although she was arguably the most famous woman poet of the Harlem Renaissance, Johnson never lived in New York and spent most of her writing life in Washington, D.C., raising her family. When her first poems came out, some black critics dismissed them as sentimental and romantic. But they praised later verses that demonstrated her race consciousness, and she began to receive greater acclaim. In both "Your World" and "Interracial," Johnson provoked a strong awareness of racial issues. In "Your World" she likened the struggles for equality to a bird finally soaring in flight; in "Interracial" she called for "bridges" to be built to close the gaps between black and white. She was stubbornly optimistic about American race relations and fought to remove prejudice, discrimination, and any other obstacles that blocked the road to opportunity.

YOUR WORLD

Your world is as big as you make it.
I know, for I used to abide
In the narrowest nest in a corner,
My wings pressing close to my side.

But I sighted the distant horizon
Where the skyline encircled the sea
And I throbbed with a burning desire
To travel this immensity.

I battered the cordons around me
And cradled my wings on the breeze,
Then soared to the uttermost reaches
With rapture, with power, with ease!

INTERRACIAL

Let's build bridges here and there
Or sometimes, just a spiral stair
That we may come somewhat abreast
And sense what cannot be exprest,
And by these measures can be found
A meeting place—a common ground
Nearer the reaches of the heart
Where truth revealed, stands clear, apart;
With understanding come to know
What laughing lips will never show:
How tears and torturing distress
May masquerade as happiness:
Then you will know when my heart's aching
And I when yours is slowly breaking.
Commune—The altars will reveal . . .
We then shall be impulsed to kneel
And send a prayer upon its way
For those who wear the thorns today.

Oh, let's build bridges everywhere
And span the gulf of challenge there.

FENTON JOHNSON

(1888–1958)

BORN INTO A WELL-TO-DO FAMILY IN A BLACK MIDDLE-CLASS NEIGHBOR-hood of Chicago, Fenton Johnson attended both Northwestern University and the University of Chicago. He first tried a teaching career but gave it up to pursue his writing. He had demonstrated his talent early, publishing his first poem by the age of twelve. His first volume of poems appeared when he was twenty-five.

Johnson married and moved to New York City in 1913, where he studied journalism at Columbia University. He began to write for newspapers and at the same time published several volumes of poetry, essays, and short stories—all before he turned thirty-three.

Johnson returned to Chicago and continued to write poems and plays, becoming involved with local theaters. During the Great Depression of the 1930s, Johnson worked for the federal government's Works Projects Administration, which brought culture and the arts to the people despite the hard times. He remained a prolific poet; a volume of his later verse was published posthumously.

~

Johnson, neither as well known nor as easy to categorize as other African American poets of his generation, spent most of his career in the Midwest. His poetry was much admired, but in 1920, his published efforts fell off dramatically. Much of his verse celebrated African American folklife in the vernacular, the spoken language of common people. Johnson also tackled political themes, as in "Children of the Sun," a powerful poem of racial protest that threatens violence and predicts the triumph of an oppressed people.

CHILDREN OF THE SUN

We are children of the sun,
     Rising sun!
Weaving Southern destiny,
Waiting for the mighty hour
When our Shiloh shall appear
With the flaming sword of right,
With the steel of brotherhood,
And emboss in crimson die
Liberty! Fraternity!

We are the star-dust folk,
     Striving folk!
Sorrow songs have lulled to rest;
Seething passions wrought through wrongs,
Led us where the moon rays dip
In the night of dull despair,
Showed us where the star gleams shine,
And the mystic symbols glow—
Liberty! Fraternity!

We have come through cloud and mist,
     Mighty men!
Dusk has kissed our sleep-born eyes,
Reared for us a mystic throne
In the splendor of the skies,
That shall always be for us,
Children of the Nazarene,
Children who shall ever sing
Liberty! Fraternity!

CLAUDE McKAY
(1890-1948)

BORN INTO A JAMAICAN FAMILY COMMITTED TO EDUCATION AND IMPROVE-ment, Claude McKay showed promise at an early age, producing two volumes of poetry before he turned twenty-one. In 1913 he came to the United States to go to school in Kansas, but he soon moved to New York City, the exciting African American literary capital and became one of the leading figures of the Harlem Renaissance. During this period, he published his most famous collection of verse, *Harlem Shadows* (1922).

McKay struggled to use his pen to advance his political agenda. He moved to England in 1919 and wrote for socialist magazines, then traveled to Russia, where his poems were translated and appeared in *Pravda*. He then settled in France for several years. His debut novel, *Home to Harlem* (1929), became the first best-seller written by an African American. McKay saw literary fame as a way to promote racial justice. In 1934 he returned to America and wrote an autobiography and a collection of essays on his adopted home of Harlem. He devoted himself to teaching and charity work after he converted to Catholicism in 1944. His death in 1948 was a major loss to the black writing community, which remained inspired by his poetic vision, his political commitment, and his literary talent.

~

Much of McKay's poetry provoked powerful and stirring responses, awakening his readers to racial injustice. McKay wrote his most famous poem, "If We Must Die," in 1919 to challenge lynching and mob violence in the South. It became known internationally when Winston Churchill read from it in a speech during World War II to enlist American support for Britain's battle against the Nazis. In his autobiography, McKay insisted that his poem "The White House" did not refer specifically to the American president's home but to all the doors that were closed by racism.

IF WE MUST DIE

If we must die, let it not be like hogs
Hunted and penned in an inglorious spot,
While round us bark the mad and hungry dogs,
Making their mock at our accursed lot.
If we must die, O let us nobly die,
So that our precious blood may not be shed
In vain; then even the monsters we defy
Shall be constrained to honor us though dead!
O kinsmen! we must meet the common foe!
Though far outnumbered let us show us brave,
And for their thousand blows deal one deathblow!
What though before us lies the open grave?
Like men we'll face the murderous, cowardly pack,
Pressed to the wall, dying, but fighting back!

THE WHITE HOUSE

Your door is shut against my tightened face,
And I am sharp as steel with discontent;
But I possess the courage and the grace
To bear my anger proudly and unbent.
The pavement slabs burn loose beneath my feet,
A chafing savage, down the decent street;
And passion rends my vitals as I pass,
Where boldly shines your shuttered door of glass.
Oh, I must search for wisdom every hour,
Deep in my wrathful bosom sore and raw,
And find in it the superhuman power
To hold me to the letter of your law!
Oh, I must keep my heart inviolate
Against the potent poison of your hate.

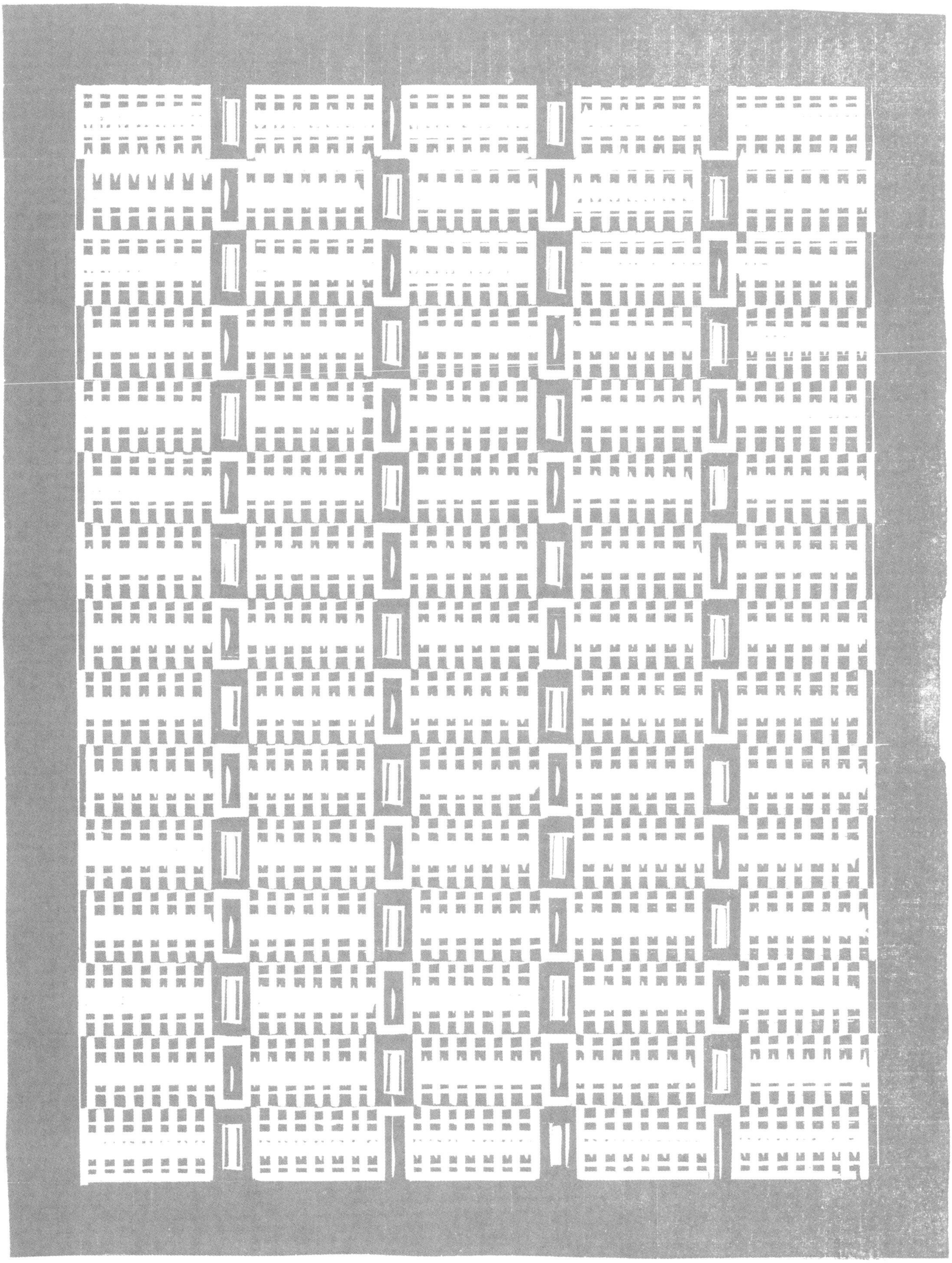

JEAN TOOMER

(1894–1967)

AN ENIGMA AMONG THE AFRICAN AMERICAN WRITERS OF HIS GENERATION, Nathan Toomer was born in Washington, D.C., to black middle-class parents. His mother divorced his father when he was only five and returned with him to her family in Louisiana, where her father had been lieutenant governor after the Civil War. Much was expected of the young Toomer.

After attending several colleges, including the University of Wisconsin, the University of Chicago, and New York University, he dropped out of school without a degree. Consumed with literary ambition, Toomer changed his first name to "Jean" in 1920 and assumed a new identity as a writer. A job in Georgia became the inspiration for his most famous work, *Cane* (1923), a collection of poetry, drama, and other sketches that received rave reviews.

Shortly thereafter, Toomer became a disciple of a Russian mystic and rejected any commitment to African American literature. He went on to publish poems and essays but never fulfilled his early promise. He once wrote, "Perhaps our lot on this earth is to seek and search," and after *Cane,* he spent his life searching. However, early critical success secured Toomer's literary influence, even after his death in 1967.

~

When it first appeared, Cane *sold only a few hundred copies. Despite its commercial failure, critics were thunderstruck by this imaginative, brilliant book, a stunning example of the richness of the Harlem Renaissance. Rural folklife in black Georgia inspired Toomer as he conjured up a beguiling world full of vivid images and powerful memories. "Beehive" is one of a series of mood pieces that draws readers into the sleepy natural beauty of the Deep South.*

BEEHIVE

Within this black hive to-night
There swarm a million bees;
Bees passing in and out of the moon,
Bees escaping out the moon,
Bees returning through the moon,
Silver bees intently buzzing,
Silver honey dripping from the swarm of bees
Earth is a waxen cell of the world comb,
And I, a drone,
Lying on my back,
Lipping honey,
Getting drunk with silver honey,
Wish that I might fly out past the moon
And curl forever in some far-off farmyard flower.

GWENDOLYN B. BENNETT

(1902-1981)

GWENDOLYN B. BENNETT WAS BORN IN TEXAS AND SPENT HER EARLY YEARS on an Indian reservation in Nevada. Her parents moved to Washington, D.C., when she was eight years old, then divorced. Although her mother gained custody, her father kidnapped her, moving from place to place and school to school until Bennett was a teenager. Despite this difficult childhood, she was a top student, pursued her artistic talent, and attended Columbia University before teaching art at Howard University. After a fellowship in Paris, she returned to New York and found a creative outlet, publishing both her poetry and illustrations in several of the black magazines that blossomed during the Harlem Renaissance. She even wrote a column for the black magazine *Opportunity*, until she and her husband, Dr. Alfred Jackson, moved to Florida in 1928. Bennett despised segregation in the South and convinced her husband to move back to Manhattan, where he died soon after. With the Depression cutting deeply into artists' lives, Bennett found her creative interests stifled. She remarried and settled in rural Pennsylvania but no longer pursued the artistic ambitions of her early years. She died in obscurity nearly fifty years after her Harlem Renaissance success.

Bennett's interest and training in fine arts gave her poetry a strong visual component. Her verses conjured up memorable images for the Harlem Renaissance—of youth, passion, and joyful high spirits. She loved dance, and her poems drew on African American cultural rhythms. In both "Heritage" and "To a Dark Girl," she celebrates the vibrant, natural beauty of black women in stark contrast to the stereotypes promoted by white segregationists. Bennett did not produce a large body of work, but with other younger artists of the Renaissance, she had a meteoric impact that helped to change attitudes toward African Americans and their cultural potential.

HERITAGE

I want to see the slim palm-trees,
Pulling at the clouds
With little pointed fingers. . . .

I want to see lithe Negro girls,
Etched dark against the sky
While sunset lingers.

I want to hear the silent sands,
Singing to the moon
Before the Sphinx-still face. . . .

I want to hear the chanting
Around a heathen fire
Of a strange black race.

I want to breathe the Lotus flow'r,
Sighing to the stars
With tendrils drinking at the Nile. . . .

I want to feel the surging
Of my sad people's soul
Hidden by a minstrel-smile.

TO A DARK GIRL

I love you for your brownness
And the rounded darkness of your breast.
I love you for the breaking sadness in your voice
And shadows where your wayward eye-lids rest.

Something of old forgotten queens
Lurks in the lithe abandon of your walk
And something of the shackled slave
Sobs in the rhythm of your talk.

Oh, little brown girl, born for sorrow's mate,
Keep all you have of queenliness,
Forgetting that you once were slave,
And let your full lips laugh at Fate!

ARNA BONTEMPS

(1902-1973)

FORCED OUT BY RACIAL VIOLENCE, BONTEMPS'S FAMILY MOVED FROM HIS birthplace of Alexandria, Louisiana, when he was three years old to Los Angeles, where the boy was given strict religious training at a boarding school. Graduating from a Seventh-Day Adventist college in 1923, he went to Harlem to teach in an Adventist academy. In 1924 Bontemps published his first poem in the *Crisis*, the magazine of the National Association for the Advancement of Colored People (NAACP). His literary reputation grew as his poems won prizes, and in 1931 he published his first novel, *God Sends Sunday*. Transferred to teach at a school in Alabama, he and his wife, Alberta, lived in Huntsville for three years. They then moved to Chicago, so Bontemps could earn a degree in library science. He was hired soon thereafter by the historically black Fisk University in Nashville, where he built Fisk into a center for African American research until his retirement in 1966. Bontemps is best remembered for his novel *Black Thunder*, the story of Gabriel's Rebellion, a slave insurrection in Richmond in 1800. He also collaborated on several projects with his great friend Langston Hughes and worked tirelessly to preserve African American culture—so much so that he has been called "the conscience of his era."

~

Bontemps's most anthologized poem, "A Black Man Talks of Reaping," reveals the historical and spiritual quality of so much of his verse. Exiled from the South as a child but returning as a mature writer, Bontemps reflects on the powerful pull of his southern roots and African American heritage. His use of metaphor and image presents a dramatic portrayal as his narrator, his everyman, speaks to the issue of black people in white America—required at the harvest, but not invited to the feast.

A BLACK MAN TALKS OF REAPING

I have sown beside all waters in my day.
I planted deep within my heart the fear
That wind or fowl would take the grain away.
I planted safe against this stark, lean year.

I scattered seed enough to plant the land
In rows from Canada to Mexico.
But for my reaping only what the hand
Can hold at once is all that I can show.

Yet what I sowed and what the orchard yields
My brother's sons are gathering stalk and root,
Small wonder then my children glean in fields
They have not sown, and feed on bitter fruit.

LANGSTON HUGHES

(1902-1967)

PERHAPS THE MOST PROLIFIC AND POPULAR WRITER OF HIS GENERATION, Langston Hughes remains widely recognized as a poet, novelist, historian, columnist, playwright, and children's author. Born in Joplin, Missouri, in 1902, he spent most of his childhood in Lawrence, Kansas, with his mother after his parents separated. In 1921 he attended Columbia University but soon left to pursue his restless ambitions: he took a tramp steamer to Africa in 1923, earned a degree at Lincoln University in Pennsylvania, and visited Haiti in 1931 and Russia in 1932. He finally returned to New York City and opened the Harlem Suitcase Theater in 1938.

In 1926 he won a prize for his poem "The Weary Blues," which launched his long and productive career as a poet. His autobiography, *The Big Sea* (1940), conveyed the significance and vibrancy of his role in the Harlem Renaissance. A prosperous and productive writer, he still had to work hard for his success and called himself a "literary sharecropper." Hughes was an outspoken advocate of racial justice, and in 1943 he launched a column for the black newspaper the *Chicago Defender* that he wrote for nearly twenty years. Hughes was dubbed "the Poet Laureate of the Negro Race" and edited several important anthologies as well as publishing nearly a dozen collections of his own poetry before his death in 1967.

Hughes published one of his most famous poems, "The Negro Speaks of Rivers" (1921), in the Crisis, *the NAACP magazine, within months of his arrival in Harlem at the age of nineteen. Another compact yet compelling poem, "Harlem," inspired the title of Lorraine Hansberry's prize-winning play* A Raisin in the Sun *in 1959. Hughes demonstrated his racial pride and cultural combativeness in his verse, which so powerfully reflected the spirit of the Harlem Renaissance. In both "Merry-Go-Round" and "I, Too, Sing America" (see Introduction), he challenged racism with his savage exposure of its ugly face. In "Cross" he tackled one of the most delicate issues of the culture: many Americans, and especially growing numbers of African Americans, share both a black and white heritage. Hughes's passion and profound sense of irony shine through in almost all his most powerful poems.*

HARLEM

What happens to a dream deferred?
Does it dry up
Like a raisin in the sun?
Or fester like a sore—
And then run?
Does it stink like rotten meat?
Or crust and sugar over—
Like a syrupy sweet?

Maybe it just sags
Like a heavy load.

Or does it explode?

THE NEGRO SPEAKS OF RIVERS

I've known rivers:
I've known rivers ancient as the world and older than the
      flow of human blood in human veins.

My soul has grown deep like the rivers.

I bathed in the Euphrates when dawns were young.
I built my hut near the Congo and it lulled me to sleep.
I looked upon the Nile and raised the pyramids above it.
I heard the singing of the Mississippi when Abe Lincoln
      went down to New Orleans, and I've seen its muddy
      bosom turn all golden in the sunset.

I've known rivers:
Ancient, dusky rivers.

My soul has grown deep like rivers.

MERRY-GO-ROUND
Colored Child at Carnival

Where is the Jim Crow section
On this merry-go-round,
Mister, cause I want to ride?
Down South where I come from
White and colored
Can't sit side by side.
Down South on the train
There's a Jim Crow car.
On the bus we're put in the back—
But there ain't no back
To a merry-go-round!
Where's the horse
For a kid that's black?

CROSS

My old man's a white old man
And my old mother's black.
If ever I cursed my white old man
I take my curses back.

If ever I cursed my black old mother
And wished she were in hell,
I'm sorry for that evil wish
And now I wish her well.

My old man died in a fine big house.
My ma died in a shack.
I wonder where I'm gonna die,
Being neither white nor black?

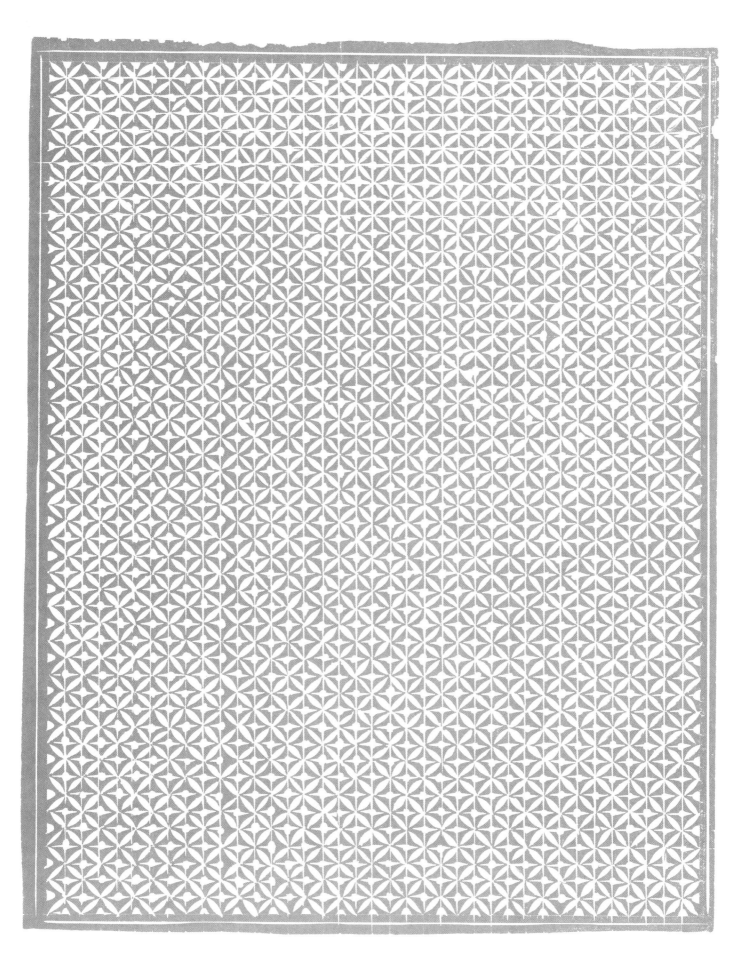

COUNTEE CULLEN

(1903–1946)

BORN IN LOUISVILLE, KENTUCKY, IN 1903, COUNTEE CULLEN WAS RAISED BY his grandmother in New York City until, at fifteen, he was adopted by an evangelical Methodist minister in Harlem. Cullen graduated in 1922 from the predominantly white DeWitt Clinton High School, where his poems appeared in its literary magazine, *The Magpie.* He attended New York University and won three years in a row a prestigious poetry prize open to all American undergraduates. He graduated with a Phi Beta Kappa key in 1925, the same year he published his first volume of verse, *Color.* Cullen went on to Harvard to earn a master's degree. Returning to New York, he published two more collections of poems in 1927: *Copper Sun* and *The Ballad of a Brown Girl.* Despite his meteoric literary rise, he was disappointed by the lack of critical enthusiasm for his collection *The Black Christ and Other Poems* (1929). Cullen had a disastrous two-year marriage to the only daughter of W. E. B. Du Bois, divorcing in 1930. He remarried in 1940 and continued to write. Forced to teach at a New York high school to support himself, he had the young James Baldwin as a student. Cullen's life was cut short tragically by illness in 1946. Perhaps Cullen's most famous lyric was: "Yet do I marvel at this curious thing / to make a poet black, and bid him sing!"

Cullen spent much of his life agonizing over his conflicting literary ambitions. To gain respect and acclaim from the white establishment, he composed ballads and sonnets to distance himself from the label "Negro poet." But he was also deeply moved by racial injustice, and many of his poems tackled important racial themes. In "Tableau," he created a sympathetic image of friendship across the color line. With "Saturday's Child," he poignantly illuminated the hardships faced by all too many African American children. His much-celebrated "Incident," which looked at racism through a child's eyes, provided a stunning indictment of bigotry.

TABLEAU

Locked arm in arm they cross the way,
    The black boy and the white,
The golden splendor of the day,
    The sable pride of night.

From lowered blinds the dark folk stare,
    And here the fair folk talk,
Indignant that these two should dare
    In unison to walk.

Oblivious to look and word
    They pass, and see no wonder
That lightning brilliant as a sword
    Should blaze the path of thunder.

SATURDAY'S CHILD

Some are teethed on a silver spoon,
    With the stars strung for a rattle;
I cut my teeth as the black raccoon—
    For implements of battle.

Some are swaddled in silk and down,
    And heralded by a star;
They swathed my limbs in a sackcloth gown
    On a night that was black as tar.

For some, godfather and goddame
    The opulent fairies be;
Dame Poverty gave me my name,
    And Pain godfathered me.

For I was born on Saturday—
    "Bad time for planting a seed,"
Was all my father had to say,
    And, "One mouth more to feed."

Death cut the strings that gave me life,
    And handed me to Sorrow,
The only kind of middle wife
    My folks could beg or borrow.

INCIDENT

For Eric Walrond

Once riding in old Baltimore,
     Heart-filled, head-filled with glee,
I saw a Baltimorean
     Keep looking straight at me.

Now I was eight and very small,
     And he was no whit bigger,
And so I smiled, but he poked out
     His tongue, and called me, "Nigger."

I saw the whole of Baltimore
     From May until December;
Of all the things that happened there
     That's all that I remember.

MARGARET WALKER

(1915-1998)

THE DAUGHTER OF A METHODIST MINISTER AND A MUSIC TEACHER, Margaret Walker was raised in a comfortable middle-class Birmingham, Alabama, home until the age of ten, when her family moved to New Orleans. She graduated from high school at fourteen and attended Dillard University, where her parents taught. When she was sixteen, she met Langston Hughes, who encouraged her to leave the South, so she transferred to Northwestern University, graduating in 1935. During the Depression, she worked for the government's Works Progress Administration in Chicago. She befriended both Langston Hughes and Richard Wright, who encouraged her to pursue her writing.

She enrolled in a creative writing program at the University of Iowa and soon began to teach and write, carving out an academic career. Three years later, Walker published her first collection of poems, *For My People*, which won the Yale University Younger Poet's Award. She moved with her family to Jackson State College in Mississippi in 1949, and taught there for the next thirty years. Walker instituted a Phillis Wheatley Festival at the college in 1973 to celebrate her African American foremother. Walker published her first novel, *Jubilee*, in 1966 and two more volumes of poetry in 1970 and in 1973. *This Is My Century: New and Collected Poetry* appeared in 1989.

~

Walker grappled with her ambivalent feelings about the South throughout her writing career. As an ambitious young black teenager, she had left her Louisiana home and headed north. Seeking a teaching post as a woman in her thirties, however, she moved to Jackson, Mississippi, her home during her most productive years. Walker captured some of her mixed feelings about her birthright as a black Southerner with her poem "Sorrow Home."

SORROW HOME

My roots are deep in southern life; deeper than John Brown
        or Nat Turner or Robert Lee. I was sired and weaned
        in a tropic world. The palm tree and banana leaf,
        mango and cocoanut, breadfruit and rubber trees
        know me.

Warm skies and gulf blue streams are in my blood. I belong
        with the smell of fresh pine, with the trail of coon,
        and the spring growth of wild onion.

I am no hot-house bulb to be reared in steam-heated flats
        with the music of "L" and subway in my ears, walled
        in by steel and wood and brick far from the sky.

I want the cotton fields, tobacco and the cane. I want to walk
        along with sacks of seed to drop in fallow ground.
        Restless music is in my heart and I am eager to be gone.

O Southland, sorrow home, melody beating in my bone and
        blood! How long will the Klan of hate, the hounds
        and the chain gangs keep me from my own?

GWENDOLYN BROOKS

(b. 1917)

THE FIRST AFRICAN AMERICAN TO WIN THE PRESTIGIOUS PULITZER PRIZE (in 1950, for poetry), Gwendolyn Brooks has had a writing career full of groundbreaking accomplishments. She was born in Kansas in 1917 but as a young girl moved to Chicago, which has remained her home ever since. She attended a predominantly white high school, then a mostly black institution, before finishing her formal education at an integrated high school and junior college in 1936. Brooks published her first poem at age thirteen, and in 1934 she began to contribute regularly to the poetry column in the *Chicago Defender*. Her mentor, Langston Hughes, encouraged her to publish her verse, and after winning a Midwestern Writers' Conference award, she published her first collection, *A Street in Bronzeville* (1945). Her next volume, *Annie Allen* (1949), earned her the Pulitzer. It was followed by several collections: first her prose poem, *Maud Martha* (1953), then *Bronzeville Boys and Girls* (1956), *The Bean Eaters* (1961), and *In the Mecca* (1968). In 1961 President John F. Kennedy asked her to read her work at a Library of Congress Poetry Festival, and in 1968 she was appointed the Poet Laureate of Illinois. Brooks claimed to have come to her art naturally: "If you wanted a poem, you had only to look out a window." She not only continues to write but conducts poetry workshops, especially for inner-city youth, to promote her philosophy that poetry should be a part of everyday life.

$$\sim$$

Brooks used her poetic gifts in her earliest collections to offer the world a view of her world in Chicago. Over time, she has become a literary figure of towering achievement who embodies African American dignity and accomplishment. The differing styles of "Martin Luther King Jr." and "Malcolm X" show her talents and reflect the contrasting styles of her subjects as well. Her poem "We Real Cool" may have come from her creative writing workshops that were attended by members of Chicago's infamous Blackstone Rangers gang.

MARTIN LUTHER KING JR.

A man went forth with gifts.

He was a prose poem.
He was a tragic grace.
He was a warm music.

He tried to heal the vivid volcanoes.
His ashes are
        reading the world.

His Dream still wishes to anoint
        the barricades of faith and of control.

His word still burns the center of the sun,
        above the thousands and the
        hundred thousands.

The word was Justice. It was spoken.

So it shall be spoken
So it shall be done.

MALCOLM X

For Dudley Randall

Original.
Ragged-round.
Rich-robust.

He had the hawk-man's eyes.
We gasped. We saw the maleness.
The maleness raking out and making guttural the air
and pushing us to walls.

And in a soft and fundamental hour
a sorcery devout and vertical
beguiled the world.

He opened us—
who was a key,

who was a man.

WE REAL COOL

The Pool Players.
Seven at the Golden Shovel.

We real cool. We
Left school. We

Lurk late. We
Strike straight. We

Sing sin. We
Thin gin. We

Jazz June. We
Die soon.

MAYA ANGELOU

(b. 1928)

WHEN MAYA ANGELOU READ "ON THE PULSE OF MORNING" AT PRESIDENT Bill Clinton's inauguration in 1993, she was the first woman poet to be so honored. She had come a long way from her difficult childhood: born in St. Louis, she suffered disruptive and painful events in her early life. She lived with her grandparents in Stamps, Arkansas, for a time, then with her mother in California as a teenager. Angelou herself became a mother at sixteen, giving birth to her son and only child. She was forced to take a series of jobs to support herself, as a waitress, cook, dancer, and actress. She was San Francisco's first black streetcar conductor, a distinction of which she remains proud. Angelou's restlessness led her to Brooklyn before she moved to Egypt, then finally, returned to the American South.

The publication of the first volume of her autobiography, *I Know Why the Caged Bird Sings* (1970), launched her career as a writer. The next year her first volume of poetry appeared, *Just Give Me a Cool Drink of Water 'Fore I Diie*. Several volumes of poetry have followed, including *And Still I Rise* (1978) and *I Shall Not Be Moved* (1990), and she continues to publish her verse. Angelou also has written for television and film. She appeared in a supporting role in Alex Haley's acclaimed television series, *Roots*, in 1977, earning an Emmy nomination. In 1981 Angelou was offered a lifetime appointment as the Reynolds Professor of American Studies at Wake Forest University, where she still lives and works.

Angelou shows her indomitable spirit, pride and fortitude in her poetry. An African American success story, and winner of a Horatio Alger Award, she believes the power of words can move a people and, against all odds, contribute to achievement and triumph. One defiant, haunting poem, "Still I Rise," symbolizes her unique voice of protest. With her regal and righteous verses, Angelou mocks oppression and defeats those who would defeat her.

STILL I RISE

You may write me down in history
With your bitter, twisted lies,
You may trod me in the very dirt
But still, like dust, I'll rise.

Does my sassiness upset you?
Why are you beset with gloom?
'Cause I walk like I've got oil wells
Pumping in my living room.

Just like moons and like suns,
With the certainty of tides,
Just like hopes springing high,
Still I'll rise.

Did you want to see me broken?
Bowed head and lowered eyes?
Shoulders falling down like teardrops,
Weakened by my soulful cries.

Does my haughtiness offend you?
Don't you take it awful hard
'Cause I laugh like I've got gold mines
Diggin' in my own back yard.

You may shoot me with your words,
You may cut me with your eyes,
You may kill me with your hatefulness,
But still, like air, I'll rise.

Does my sexiness upset you?
Does it come as a surprise
That I dance like I've got diamonds
At the meeting of my thighs?

Out of the huts of history's shame
I rise
Up from a past that's rooted in pain
I rise
I'm a black ocean, leaping and wide,
Welling and swelling I bear in the tide.

Leaving behind nights of terror and fear
I rise
Into a daybreak that's wondrously clear
I rise
Bringing the gifts that my ancestors gave,
I am the dream and the hope of the slave.
I rise
I rise
I rise.

AUDRE LORDE

(1934-1992)

BORN IN HARLEM, AUDRE LORDE DID NOT SPEAK UNTIL SHE WAS FIVE YEARS old, and she continued to have difficulty communicating orally throughout her childhood. She attended Catholic schools and, encouraged to express herself through writing, composed her first poem when she was in the eighth grade. Later she worked as a medical clerk and X-ray technician to support herself while she attended Hunter College in Manhattan, graduating in 1959. She studied in Mexico for a year before earning her master's degree in library science from Columbia University in 1961. Her writing career took off in 1968 when her debut collection of poems, *The First Cities*, was published, and she was invited to be a poet-in-residence at Tougaloo College, a small black college in Mississippi. Although she had married and given birth to two children before her divorce in 1970, it was also around this time that Lorde began to refer to her emerging lesbian identity. Her many collections of poetry received growing acclaim, and she was nominated for a National Book Award. Admired for her courageous struggle with illness, she published *The Cancer Journals* in 1980. Her most influential book, *Sister Outsider: Essays and Speeches* (1984), turned her into a cult heroine. Lorde was completing *Undersong: Chosen Poems Old and New* when she died of cancer in 1992.

Coming of age during the Black Arts movement of the 1960s, Lorde wrote for the masses, not the critics, and she portrayed a sense of being an "outsider." Throughout her life, Lorde was engaged in a struggle—to overcome hardships as a child, poverty as a young adult, prejudice as a black lesbian woman, and her own terminal illness. In "Rites of Passage," she grapples with the way generations strive for improved lives, propelled by the love of their children, who remind them not to forget their dreams.

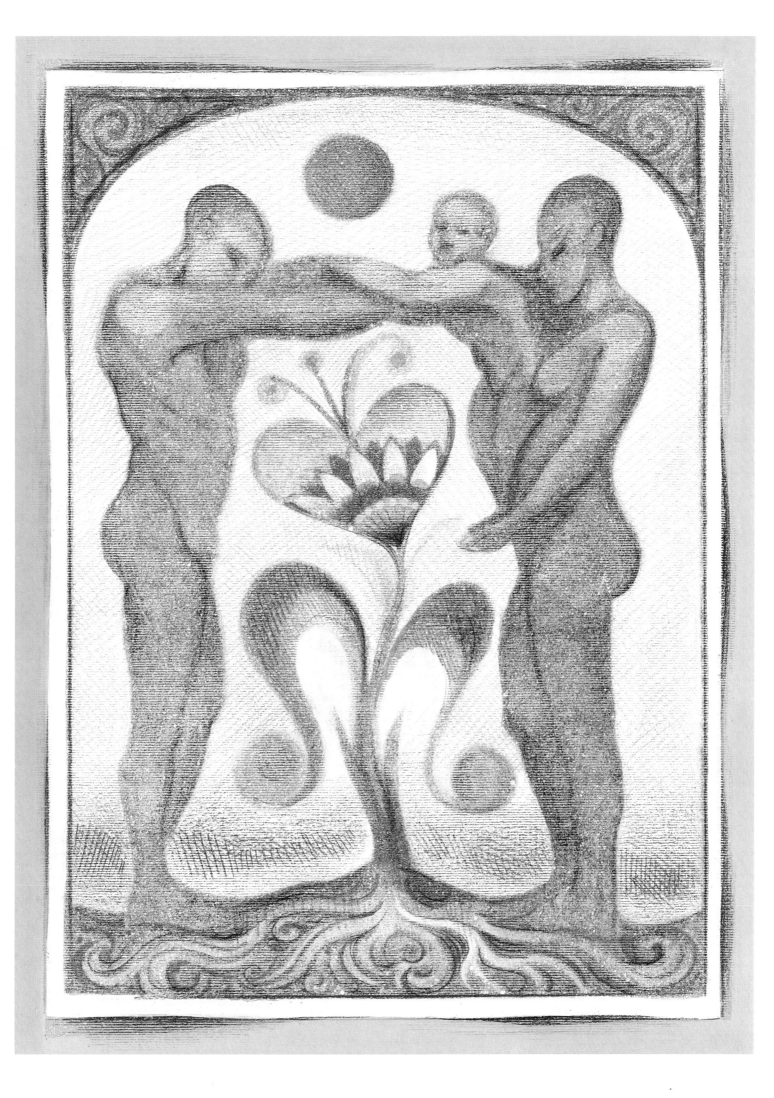

RITES OF PASSAGE

Now rock the boat to a fare-thee-well.
Once we suffered dreaming
into the place where the children are playing
their child's games
where the children are hoping
knowledge survives if
unknowing
they follow the game
without winning.

Their fathers are dying
back to the freedom of wise children
playing at knowing
their fathers are dying
whose deaths will not free them
of growing from knowledge
of knowing
when the game becomes foolish
a dangerous pleading
for time out of power.

Quick
children kiss us
we are growing
through dream.

AMIRI BARAKA

(b. 1934)

AMIRI BARAKA WAS BORN EVERETT LEROI JONES, THE SON OF COMFORTABLE middle-class parents in Newark, New Jersey. He graduated from high school at fifteen and in 1952 entered Howard University, but soon he dropped out and joined the U.S. Air Force. He then moved to Greenwich Village in New York City, where he became part of the literary scene and was nicknamed "King of the Village." In 1959 Baraka published "January 1 1959: Fidel Castro" which earned him an invitation to Cuba, where he was inspired by the revolutionaries and intellectuals he encountered. He published his first collection of poems, *Cuba Libre*, in 1961. Fervently embracing black nationalism, he changed his name to Amiri Baraka. After the 1965 assassination of Malcolm X, whom Baraka greatly admired, he moved to Harlem and founded the Black Arts Repertory School to promote racial pride and black activism. In 1966 Baraka returned to Newark, where he was a political organizer, an educator, and a leading light of the Black Arts Movement in the 1960s. He went on to edit *Black Fire: An Anthology of Afro-American Writing* (1968), which highlighted the dynamism of African American literary culture, especially that of young writers. Baraka has continued to exert a remarkable influence as an author and intellectual, becoming both a prize-winning playwright (for his drama *Dutchman*) and a leading African American scholar at Rutgers University.

Many of Baraka's poems are fueled by events within the African American community as well as larger issues involving race and class. As an artist committed to social change, Baraka often illuminates political injustice, demands for black autonomy, and commitment to activism. In his poem "In the Year," he harps on themes recurrent in his work: the oppressiveness of American racism, the need for collective action, the value of historical consciousness, and the power of self-reliance for blacks in carving out a future.

IN THE YEAR

In the year of reconstruction, 1969, we turn again
to look at our selves, turn again to old understanding
experience colors the landscape reality color, curtains of words
trap dreams like objects
a suicide name America
breathes farts on our momentary conclusions
so turn again
rear up again
the thing we need, is each other
if we could find completion as sand lays cool for the rising
wave
a natural
dependence
on what already exists

though the tide returns each night
and the earth speeds through space
they hook up just the same

NIKKI GIOVANNI

(b. 1943)

NIKKI GIOVANNI WAS BORN IN KNOXVILLE, TENNESSEE, AND WAS RAISED BY her parents in Cincinnati, though she spent summers with her grandparents back in Knoxville and eventually attended high school there. She enrolled at Fisk University, where she took writing workshops and participated in the Student Nonviolent Coordinating Committee, a radical civil rights group. Giovanni headed north for graduate school in 1967, first to the University of Pennsylvania and then to Columbia, where she was a champion of the Black Arts Movement. She gave birth to a son in the same year William Morrow published a collection of her poems, *Black Feeling, Black Talk/Black Judgment* (1970). The following year she recorded her verses accompanied by gospel music, *Truth Is on Its Way*, an album that attracted a wide audience and launched her on a successful career. Her early work was characterized by strident militancy, but her publication of a book of love poems, *My House* (1972), signaled a new direction. Her collections of poetry for both adults and children combine her introspective thoughts and her ongoing commitment to social and political activism. She has been awarded more than ten honorary degrees and remains a dynamic role model for aspiring young writers.

~

Giovanni has earned legions of fans as an outspoken black woman poet for more than thirty years. She remains committed to the African American heritage of combining verse and music. Her meditation "The Funeral of Martin Luther King, Jr." was one of the many tributes that poured forth following the civil rights leader's assassination. Giovanni and her fellow mourners demonstrated King's historic role as an advocate of nonviolence and social justice.

THE FUNERAL OF MARTIN LUTHER KING, JR.

His headstone said
FREE AT LAST, FREE AT LAST
But death is a slave's freedom
We seek the freedom of free men
And the construction of a world
Where Martin Luther King could have lived
and preached non-violence

ALICE WALKER

(b. 1944)

WHEN SHE WON THE PULITZER PRIZE FOR FICTION FOR *THE COLOR PURPLE* in 1982, Alice Walker was the first African American woman to be so honored. Born in Eatonton, Georgia, she lost the sight in her right eye after a childhood accident with a BB gun. Walker overcame her partial blindness to graduate as valedictorian from her high school class. She spent two years at Spelman, a black women's college in Atlanta, before completing her education at Sarah Lawrence College, graduating in 1965. Two years later Walker married a Jewish civil rights lawyer and moved to Jackson, Mississippi, where she gave birth to a daughter and became active in the civil rights movement. In 1968 she published her first book of poems, *Once*, soon followed by *Five Poems* (1970). Her third collection, *Revolutionary Petunias and Other Poems* (1973), was nominated for a National Book Award and won the Lillian Smith Award, a prize that recognizes both literary merit and social impact. During this period Walker began to write fiction. Her first novel appeared in 1970, and a little over a decade later she won both the National Book Award and the Pulitzer Prize for *The Color Purple*. Her collected essays, *In Search of Our Mother's Gardens* (1974), chronicled her heroic efforts to rediscover the neglected Harlem Renaissance writer Zora Neale Hurston—like Walker, the daughter of sharecroppers. Walker continues to write and has been a distinguished visiting professor at many prestigious universities, including Yale. In 1997 the Alice Walker Literary Society was founded in Georgia.

Though perhaps better known for her novels, Walker is an award-winning poet as well. In one of her earliest published poems, "Women," she pays tribute to the women whose struggles paved the way for her own success. Denied access to opportunities in education, Walker's foremothers nevertheless provided powerful role models for her as a writer, and she celebrated their strengths.

WOMEN

They were women then
My mama's generation
Husky of voice—Stout of
Step
With fists as well as
Hands
How they battered down
Doors
And ironed
Starched white
Shirts
How they led
Armies
Headragged Generals
Across mined
Fields
Booby-trapped
Ditches
To discover books
Desks
A place for us
How they knew what we
Must know
Without knowing a page
Of it
Themselves.

RITA DOVE

(b. 1952)

RAISED IN HER BIRTHPLACE OF AKRON, OHIO, RITA DOVE GAINED A DEEP AND abiding appreciation of education from her parents. A gifted student, she was encouraged to pursue her literary talents. As a senior in high school, she was named a Presidential Scholar and invited to the White House. She graduated with honors from Miami University in 1973, then studied in West Germany on a Fulbright Scholarship before earning a creative writing degree in 1977 from the University of Iowa. There she met her husband, a novelist, with whom she has a daughter. She published a short chapbook of verse, *Ten Poems* (1977), and received a National Endowment for the Arts award the following year. Her first major collection of poetry, *The Yellow House on the Corner*, appeared in 1980. Joining the faculty of Arizona State University, she began her association with an African American arts journal, *Callaloo*. In 1987 she won the Pulitzer Prize for poetry for her moving narrative, *Thomas and Beulah* (1986). Following several prestigious fellowships, including a Mellon Award and a Rockefeller grant, Dove moved to the University of Virginia. She was invited in 1993 to be the poet laureate of the United States, the youngest ever and the first African American offered this honor. Dove remains a prolific and popular writer, publishing short stories, plays, and a novel, and continues to receive many honors, including a Guggenheim Award, a Walt Whitman Award, and an international prize in honor of Carl Sandburg.

~

Dove's spunk and determination from an early age, as much as her enormous talent, drove her career as an award-winning writer. In "Primer," we can glimpse the grit and joy that propelled her to succeed. Only the second black woman to win a Pulitzer Prize in poetry, Dove described one of her collections as a labor of love, where she tried to "string moments as beads on a necklace."

PRIMER

In the sixth grade I was chased home by
the Gatlin kids, three skinny sisters
in rolled-down bobby socks. Hissing
Brainiac! and *Mrs. Stringbean!*, they trod my heel.
I knew my body was no big deal
but never thought to retort: who's
calling *who* skinny? (Besides, I knew
they'd beat me up.) I survived
their shoves across the schoolyard
because my five-foot-zero mother drove up
in her Caddie to shake them down to size.
Nothing could get me into that car.
I took the long way home, swore
I'd show them all: I would grow up.

Editor's Note

Sitting cross-legged on a classroom floor in 1996, watching a row of first-graders, my own son included, reciting one of Langston Hughes's poems, I was moved by the simple beauty of their encounter with poetry. This incident brought back memories of my mother reading me the poems of Paul Laurence Dunbar when I was a child, and propelled me along a path to undertake this volume. The stories of the poets, as well as the stories they tell, are an important part of my commitment to this project. Along with my talented collaborator, Stephen Alcorn, who evokes the very souls of these verses, I hope our selections will touch the imagination of our readers the way they have inspired us.

—Catherine Clinton

Illustrator's Note

Thematically, *I, Too, Sing America: Three Centuries of African American Poetry* is the natural outgrowth of a large body of work I've done within the context of the African American experience, ranging from the trials and tribulations of nineteenth-century America to the life and times of Langston Hughes. Both technically and stylistically, however, this volume represents a departure for me. Whereas my previous work is characterized by the dramatic use of one- and two-color relief-block prints, this volume instead embraces the realm of lush color—a fitting home for the vivid imaginations celebrated throughout these pages.

Just as the words of these poems were designed to resonate and to transcend their inherent economy of means, so too is my use of color in these images. In the case of verse, two words often serve to evoke a third word. Similarly, in the world of color, when two colors are placed judiciously side by side, they can serve to suggest a third vibrant hue, if only in the eye of the beholder. To accomplish this, colors, like words, require room within which to breathe.

My impassioned collaborator, Catherine Clinton, has cast a revealing beam of light onto the poets and their lives, thus gracing this book with a sense of balanced symmetry, at the center of which lie the poems themselves.

—Stephen Alcorn